Waylon!
The Most Awesome of All

Waylon!
The Most Awesome of All

SARA PENNYPACKER

PICTURES BY
Marla Frazee

DISNEP • HYPERION
Los Angeles   New York

A special thank-you to Daniel Shintaku for hand-writing our endpapers

First Edition, April 2019
1 3 5 7 9 10 8 6 4 2
FAC-020093-19074
Printed in the United States of America

This book is set in 13-point Garth Graphic Regular-Monotype
Designed by Michelle Gengaro-Kokmen
Illustrations created in Black Verithin pencil on Dura-lar polyester film

Library of Congress Cataloging-in-Publication Data

Names: Pennypacker, Sara, 1951- author. • Frazee, Marla, illustrator.
Title: Waylon! : the most awesome of all / Sara Pennypacker ; pictures by
    Marla Frazee.
Description: First edition. • Los Angeles ; New York : Disney-Hyperion, 2019.
Summary: Waylon gives up a chance to meet a famous astrophysicist to help his sister,
his father, and a friend when they need him most, but gains a much greater reward.
Identifiers: LCCN 2017004989 • ISBN 9781484701546
Subjects: • CYAC: Performance art—Fiction. • Helpfulness—Fiction. •
    Secrets—Fiction. • Family life—Fiction. • Dogs—Fiction.
Classification: LCC PZ7.P3856 Wbm 2016 • DDC [Fic]—dc23
LC record available at https://lccn.loc.gov/2017004989

Reinforced binding
Visit www.DisneyBooks.com

For the crew at NASA. You GO!
—S.P.

To the Shintaku family—Janice,
Mike, Matt, Jenny, David,
and especially Daniel
—M.F.

1

Waylon rushed into the condo, starving as usual. In one practiced motion, he slipped his right arm out of his backpack, dropped the keys on the counter, and reached for the cupboard handle.

There he froze, his eye caught by the wall calendar. His jaw fell open. He'd never witnessed a complete, four-ring target on it before. Two circles around the same date were rare enough, and three had happened only a few times in his life.

He traced the circles to be sure. Yep, outside the third ring around June 14—which was in green, his own color—there was now a *fourth*. In purple, his mother's color.

His backpack dropped to the floor. "All four," he marveled out loud.

"Oh, hi, buddy," his father called out from his writing studio. "All four what?"

Waylon didn't answer. He found a bag of pretzels, ripped it open, and started eating. His mother hadn't written anything beside her circle. That was odd.

Waylon felt his father join him at the calendar. He glanced over. Mr. Zakowski was wearing the same ratty pajamas he'd worn for days, and his hair had a dangerous look, as if it would shoot off and commit mayhem if it weren't rooted at the follicles.

Lately Waylon's father had been a bit

preoccupied, working on the final draft of his
screenplay. Little things like personal hygiene
kept getting forgotten.

"How's it coming?" Waylon asked. "Did you
finish?"

Mr. Zakowski frowned and shook his head.
"Now, all four what?"

Waylon pointed a pretzel toward the calendar. "What's Mom doing next Thursday?"

Looking at the date, Mr. Zakowski grew pale. Waylon realized his mistake. His dad's gaze was fixed on the center circle, the one in red. He had set this date exactly two years before, on his fortieth birthday, when he'd marched out of his office at the accounting firm and given himself twenty-four months to sell a screenplay. He had vowed that if he didn't succeed by June 14, he'd cinch a tie around his neck and drag himself back to that office.

Waylon's dad clutched his throat as if he could already feel that necktie strangling him. "The final scene," he choked out, "lacks pizzazz. . . ." And then he backed into his writing studio and started typing.

Just then, the front door burst open and Waylon's sister stormed in. "Neon," Waylon asked, "do you know what Mom's doing on—?"

Neon plowed past him, snatching the bag of pretzels on her way. She yanked open the refrigerator and slammed a cup of yogurt onto the counter.

Waylon tried again. "Do you know why Mom circled—?"

Neon shot a silencing palm at his face. "Creating," she warned.

Waylon sighed. Ever since she'd gotten the letter informing her she'd won third prize in the New Voices in Boston Theater contest and could stage her performance at the Beantown Repertory Theater, Neon had grown more Neon-y than usual. This past week she'd become absolutely savage. He waited as she stabbed pretzel after pretzel into her yogurt and stuffed them into her mouth, her face screwed into a fierce scowl.

When she dropped the empty yogurt cup and slumped over the counter, he tried once more. "It's the same day as your play and my—"

Again, he got the palm. "Not a play—a *performance*." Then she wailed, "My performance! Quiet! Thinking . . ."

Waylon knew when to give up. He recaptured the pretzel bag and called good-bye to his father. "I'm going to go play with Eddy. I'll do my homework after dinner."

Before he got to the door, though, Neon had stomped over to the calendar. "Wait!" she ordered. "How many can you round up?"

"How many what?"

"Bodies," Neon said. "I'll even take fourth graders."

"What for?"

Neon rolled her eyes. "My performance. I asked everyone in my class and only got eleven. The show is about abundance. I need an abundancier number of people." She jabbed the circle in black—her color. The bull's-eye. "I have exactly one week to assemble the cast, hold rehearsals, and build all the scenery. How about your mini-cop friend?"

"Baxter? You want Baxter?"

Neon nodded. "Besides being on the stage, he can handle crowd control. The audience will probably go crazy when they see this production. Bring him. Oh, and who was that kid who directed your talent show last year? Red haired, bossed everyone around?"

"Clementine?"

Neon got a faraway look in her eye. "That kid had a real talent for it. And not just with little kids. She had those grown-ups jumping, too—the janitor, the teacher who was running the lights, even the principal."

"Clementine's not bossy. Except with her little brother."

Neon smiled dreamily. "Yeah. That kid reminds me of myself at that age. Bring her."

"Okay, I'll ask them. But they might not want to come, you know." Waylon reached for the doorknob.

"And your dog. Of course."

Waylon stopped. "Eddy?"

"Your dog. The one you're always going on about—you know, how awesome he is."

"Why do you want him? I mean, Eddy *is* awesome. But what's he going to do?"

Neon fired a look of disbelief. "Hel-*lo*? *The Everything* is about *everything*. He can represent the animal kingdom."

Waylon hurried out of the condo. His whole

family had gone nuts lately. His sister with her performance, his father with his looming dead-line, and his mother . . . Come to think of it, he had barely even seen his mother lately.

Luckily there was still someone in his world he could count on.

2

Dumpster Eddy leaped out of his basket in a manic frenzy the instant Waylon opened the police station door. "Hold on, hold on," Waylon called. "You know the drill."

The drill was: before Waylon and Eddy could greet each other, Waylon put on the old garage mechanic's suit he kept at the police station. This was to keep Eddy's hairs from coming home to his condo. Waylon's mom was so allergic, even a few hairs could set her off.

When Waylon had gotten himself zipped up, Eddy flew across the room and jumped into his arms. You'd think that Waylon had spent the hours since Eddy had last seen him in the middle of the Indian Ocean—latitude: 42° 21' 36.3" S, longitude: 108° 56' 28" E—instead of just a few blocks away.

The middle of the Indian Ocean—latitude: 42° 21' 36.3" S, longitude: 108° 56' 28" E— was the antipode of Waylon's home in Boston, Massachusetts. The antipode of a location is the exact place on Earth opposite that location.

Waylon really enjoyed thinking about antipodes, especially when he imagined them this way: if he happened to drop a slice of bread at home, and someone at latitude X, longitude Y happened to drop a slice of bread at the same time, they'd make a perfect Earth sandwich.

Of course, Waylon knew that an Earth sandwich would be too hot to eat, because the planet's core is about 10,800 degrees. But still, he smiled whenever he imagined it.

"Take it easy, boy, take it easy!" Waylon said as Eddy slurped his face. Although he understood his dog's excitement. It had rained in the morning, but now the sky was scrubbed a bright blue. It was as if Eddy knew there were puddles waiting for him to splash in, trash cans for him to explore, and squirrels for him to chase on the way to the park. Waylon snapped on Eddy's red leash. "Let's get out of here!"

Waylon and Eddy shot out of the station

into that perfect June day, and, sure enough, there *were* puddles to splash in and trash cans to explore, and squirrels to chase on the way to the park.

Once they were there, the afternoon got even better.

After Eddy had sniffed every square inch of the park, reading news of who had been there since his last visit, Waylon called out, "Dog Olympics!" Eddy took off like a shot for the

hundred-yard dash, flying around the chain-link perimeter in record time. He hurdled two park benches cleanly and made a dramatic improvement in his standing vertical vault, leaping so high Waylon didn't have to bend at all to catch him.

Eddy's friend Oscar, a border collie, showed up, and for a while, Waylon watched the two of them romp. Eddy seemed every bit as happy and healthy as Oscar was, and Waylon knew

Oscar had been pampered from the time he was a puppy. Dumpster Eddy had come a long way this year, and Waylon was proud of that.

But then Waylon's watch alarm beeped—that beep was the saddest sound in the world—and Waylon leashed Eddy and walked him back.

At the police station, he scooped a can of Happy Pup into the dish so he could leave without Eddy howling his head off. Dumpster Eddy hated their good-byes.

Waylon hated their good-byes, too. He peeled off the jumpsuit and slipped out without looking back.

"I'm so lucky," he reminded himself out loud, over and over, walking home.

And it was true. He *was* lucky. Just last year, he hadn't had a dog at all. The situation had seemed hopeless. His mother was dangerously allergic to dogs, and that was the way things were going to stay. Forever.

And then, the string of miracles! In the fall, he'd met Dumpster Eddy, the most wonderful dog in the world. He and Baxter had managed to rescue him from Dog Death Row at the shelter time after time by setting him free. In January, the police had said okay, Eddy could live in their station as long as Waylon took care of him.

So now he had a dog. Waylon could play with him and teach him tricks and hug him every single day, just like any regular kid and his dog.

Almost.

It wasn't perfect.

The truth was, Waylon wished more than anything that he could bring Eddy home.

He wanted his dog to be part of the family.

He wanted him to beg for scraps from under the table; to make a big pretend-fierce racket whenever anyone knocked at the door; to curl up on the couch with everybody on movie night.

Mostly, he wished he could call Eddy into his room. At bedtime, Waylon's room felt empty, as if it were missing a dog bed. His bed felt empty, too, as if it were missing a dog who would sneak out of that dog bed and burrow down under the covers with him. Worst of all, Waylon's body felt empty, as if it were missing an important organ.

"I am so lucky!" he ordered himself to remember again out loud. "And also so hungry!"

The pretzels were long gone, and Waylon was ravenous again. Lately, it seemed he was constantly starving. He'd grown two inches already this year, and the year wasn't even half-over. His eleventh birthday was coming up at the end of the month, and sometimes it felt as if his eleven-year-old self were a caterpillar ready to burst out of his ten-year-old-Waylon skin.

He started to run, thinking about dinner. But as he turned the corner to his block, he skidded to a stop.

3

A shiny blue car was parked in the Drop-Off Only space in front of his condo building. Waylon didn't recognize this car or the blond man behind its wheel, but he did recognize his mother's green raincoat getting out.

Waylon watched as his mother bent to the backseat window. A little boy's blond head popped out, and Waylon's mother tapped his nose with her fingertip. She leaned in and said something to another golden-haired head in the backseat. Then she waved and ran up the condo steps.

Even from this distance, Waylon could see she was smiling.

He hurried to the crosswalk, and as he waited for the light, he pondered the mystery of what he'd just seen.

Mrs. Zakowski always took the subway to and from her lab. Always.

Waylon didn't like mysteries. He liked knowing things.

The light changed, and he sprinted across the street and up the stairs to his condo.

Mrs. Zakowski was at the coat hooks.

"Hi, Mom, how come you didn't take the subway, who gave you a ride, and if someone gave you a ride, how come you're home later instead of earlier?" Waylon demanded in one breath.

Waylon's mom stepped out of her shoes. "Did you have a nice afternoon with your dog?"

"Mom! Who's the blond family in the shiny blue car?"

Waylon's mom looked at the clock. "You're right. I am a little late. We should get dinner started."

Waylon grabbed her hand. "And what's this?" he asked, dragging her over to the calendar.

"How come you circled Thursday? You remember you've got to drive me to the Expo Center that day, right? I need to be there by four. We need to go straight from school. Remember, Dr. Geller—"

"I remember, I remember, don't worry," Mrs. Zakowski said. "It's also a pretty important day for your sister, you know. I wouldn't do anything to miss her play."

"Not a play—a *performance!*" Neon's voice thundered from her room.

Waylon hung his head. He felt bad about missing Neon's performance. But it wasn't his fault the Boston Science Expo was on the same night. Mrs. Resnick had said it was a huge honor for the whole school that his project had been chosen—he couldn't let down the whole school, could he? And besides . . . Dr. Margaret J. Geller!!!

"But, wait," Waylon said. "What's your circle *for?*"

Mrs. Zakowski turned to the calendar. "My goodness. I just circled that this morning. It's amazing you noticed such a tiny thing."

"No, it isn't," Waylon said. "Humans are wired to notice slight changes, the things that are different."

"Interesting. Do you know why?"

Waylon did. He'd read about it in his favorite book—*The Science of Being Human,* Chapter Three, "Your Inner Caveman." "It's a survival trait passed on from our hunting ancestors," he explained. "When you're hungry, you can't waste time processing the billions of blades of grass waving in the wind. No, you want to pick out the few that are moving differently because a warthog is lumbering through. Then it's warthog for dinner."

"Oh, so you were hungry this afternoon. Looking for warthog maybe?"

"No. I wasn't looking for anything! Mom, what's your circle for?"

"Really? You weren't looking for anything to eat? Because lately you've been a bottomless pit."

"Well," Waylon admitted, "maybe I was hoping there was butterscotch pudding. But—"

"Butterscotch pudding," Mrs. Zakowski said. "We'll see if there's time to make some. For now, go set the table for dinner while I change out of my lab clothes."

Only much later, lying in bed feeling disappointed because there hadn't been any butterscotch pudding for dessert after all, Waylon realized what his mother had done. With all her questions about survival traits and warthogs and pudding, she had thrown him off track.

28

She was keeping a secret. That thought made him feel way worse than no butterscotch pudding for dessert.

4

"Mr. Zakowski, pay attention!"

The first time Mrs. Fernman yelled those words Friday morning, Waylon had jumped in shock: was she talking to *him*?

The second time, he'd felt his cheeks burn.

The third time, a growl rumbled up his throat. He gritted his teeth to keep it from escaping.

Clementine turned around in her seat with a sympathetic smile.

Suddenly, he knew how Clementine must have felt all the times Mrs. Fernman had called her out for the same thing. Clementine had always argued that she *had* been paying attention, and now Waylon understood that, too.

Because Waylon had been paying attention all morning.

He'd been paying attention to the mystery of his mother's behavior. What was she hiding, and why?

He'd been paying attention to the problem of how to convince Baxter and Clementine to be in Neon's performance. Waylon felt guilty enough not being in it himself; he didn't want to let Neon down more by not supplying some bodies.

Mostly, though, he'd been paying attention to the daydream that had been obsessing him for months now. *That's quite a science project, young man,* Dr. Geller was likely to say when she walked past Waylon's display at the Expo. *I can see you're a science-y person, like myself.* The question was, what to say in response? And she was a science-y person all right—she was the astrophysicist mapping the universe!

All of these things were *way* more important than *Stack your workbooks alphabetically for collection next week* and *Don't forget your sneakers on Field Day.*

Waylon riveted his attention on Mrs. Fernman. He crossed his eyes slightly, and hung his mouth open in a look of spellbound fascination. Finally the noon bell rang, and the class clattered out to the lunchroom.

At the table, Waylon dropped his tray next to Baxter's and called Clementine over. "My sister wants you both to be in her performance at the Rep next week. Rehearsal starts today."

He stuffed a couple of chicken nuggets into his mouth, hoping neither friend would ask what Neon's performance was about, or what they'd have to do onstage.

"What's her performance about?" Baxter asked.

"What do I have to do onstage?" Clementine demanded.

The chicken nuggets congealed into a throat-clogging clump. Waylon swallowed hard. "I don't know," he admitted. He rested his forehead in his palms as he waited for his friends to say *No thanks . . . Sounds awful . . . Don't bother us again.*

"Okay, fine," said Clementine. "I can't come today, but I'll be there tomorrow."

"I can come today," said Baxter. "I just need to stop by the station first and tell my dad."

So after school, Baxter walked with Waylon to the police station. After being thoroughly licked by Dumpster Eddy, Baxter took off to look for Officer Boylen.

Waylon wriggled into his jumpsuit and then found the dispatcher in the break room. "How's Eddy been at night?" he asked her. "Has the howling gotten better?"

The dispatcher poured herself some coffee and took a sip, thinking. "About the same.

He's fine if I can hold him and rub his ears until he gets sleepy. But I'm usually too busy. Sorry."

Waylon thanked her again for taking such good care of his dog at night. Then Baxter came back, and they leashed up Eddy and left for the theater.

Eddy led the way, sprinting from tree to tree in search of squirrels. "You're supposed to represent the whole animal kingdom in Neon's thing," Waylon warned him as the dog tried to scramble up yet another trunk. "That probably includes squirrels."

Waylon thought about it. "Actually, I don't know what Neon's expecting you to do. But don't worry. If it's something embarrassing, I'll pull you out," he promised.

He looked up at Baxter. "You too, of course," he added in a hurry. "If Neon makes you do anything too weird, I'll—"

Baxter just waved him away, as though he didn't care about being embarrassed.

Waylon looked at his watch. "Rehearsal starts in fifteen minutes," he said, giving a little tug on Eddy's leash. "My sister isn't the kind of director you can be late for."

"Hey, I can take Eddy there myself," Baxter offered. "Then you don't have to waste your afternoon."

Waylon shook his head. "It's okay, I don't mind."

Actually, Waylon liked visiting the Beantown Rep. His father picked up odd jobs there on weekends—lighting, sound effects, costuming the actors. Since Waylon enjoyed tagging along with his father to these jobs, he'd made some friends in the old theater.

His favorite was an actress named Marliana Versala.

Marliana always carried macaroons in her tote bag. *There's nothing better for when I bomb at an audition,* she'd explained. *Have one.*

Waylon pulled Eddy off the trail of another squirrel and trotted him on a short leash the rest of the way. At the theater, he led Baxter and Eddy to the back entrance. He pulled open the old red door, and as his eyes adjusted to

the dark, he drew in the familiar scents: paint, makeup, and fresh-cut plywood.

None of these smells were familiar to Dumpster Eddy, though. When Waylon unsnapped his leash, Eddy lowered his snout and took off. Baxter and Waylon followed him past the dressing rooms, past the costume storage, past the orchestra equipment, and up the stairs to the back of the stage.

There, Waylon and Baxter stopped in their tracks to gape.

5

___

An enormous curved horn towered over the stage.

The enormous curved horn didn't stop Eddy in his tracks. He shot across the stage and long-jumped into Neon's arms as if he'd known her forever. Neon laughed, and then nuzzled Eddy's bony head as if she'd known him forever, too.

Waylon and Baxter walked up to the horn. The wide end rested on the wooden floor, the opening at least six feet across. Aluminum steps led up to the smaller opening, seven feet in the air. A couple of kids from Neon's class were bending chicken wire over the structure, and two girls were slapping wads of papier-mâché over the frame.

Neon put Eddy down and turned to the two girls. "Lay it on a little thicker," she instructed.

"What's that?" Waylon asked, pointing to the horn.

"Cornucopia." Neon smoothed some of the wet paste onto its side, then wiped her hands on her tights.

Up close, Waylon realized that the cornucopia had been built around a playground slide. "What's it for?"

"Stage entrance," Neon answered. "The actors will slide down through it onto the stage."

"How come?" Waylon asked.

Neon smirked as if this were the dumbest question in the universe. "A cornucopia signifies abundance. . . . Get it?"

Waylon pictured the cornucopias he'd seen on Thanksgiving cards. "Won't everyone come out all sticky, sliding through grapes and stuff? Eddy wouldn't mind that, but the others—"

"Not *through* abundance. The actors *are* the abundance! Everyone is part of the abundance of life!"

Now Waylon was truly confused. He pointed at Baxter. "*He's* abundance? *Dumpster Eddy* is abundance?"

"Of course. It's symbolism. Now get out of here—we have work to do. Come back at five for your dog."

"Nuh-uh," Waylon said, hopping off the stage. "I'm staying to watch this. Eddy, stay with Baxter."

Halfway down the aisle, he recognized a familiar shape in the darkened theater.

Marliana waved, and Waylon made his way to the back row and dropped down beside her.

Marliana leaned in and pointed to Eddy, who was sniffing at the bucket of paste beside the cornucopia. "So that's the famous Dumpster Eddy," she whispered. "Some dog!"

Waylon thanked her, and then they fell silent to watch what was happening onstage.

Neon attached a roll of toilet paper to the back of each kid's shirt, and tied another one

44

to Eddy's collar. She freed the end from each roll and taped it to the floor. "Okay," she said. "Now it will unroll as you move, leaving a trail of where you've been. My dad will be in the middle of the floor, next to the cornucopia, acting out the stages of human life. He can't be here today, so we'll use this coatrack—pretend it's him. Every time you cross the stage, loop your streamer around him."

"But what are we supposed to do?" asked one kid. "Just cross the stage?"

Neon nodded. "The abundance of life is random. Random encounters with random souls. Just wander around the stage, and whenever you bump into someone, have an encounter. Silently. Anisha will be in the balcony with a red flashlight. If she shines it on you, you talk. If not, you're silent."

"An encounter?" Baxter asked. "Like what?"

"I'll leave it up to you—it's called *improv*. Buy some groceries from one, have an argument with another. Hug one, play a game with another. You know, life. Oh, and there will be lights and music and weather going on, too, so react to that. But today, just practice the encountering."

The kids shrugged at each other, but pretty soon they started wandering around the stage. Baxter went police-y in his encounters: he

helped one kid cross an imaginary street, bought some imaginary doughnuts from a second, and put the rest in imaginary handcuffs.

The best actor by far was Dumpster Eddy. He scrambled around, encountering like crazy, leaving a mad tangle of streamers crisscrossing the stage.

"What's with the toilet paper?" one girl asked as she looped hers around a coatrack arm.

"It's a visible representation of the connections we all make. My dad, in the center, will be totally webbed by the end. The audience will see the trails that represent all the ways he's connected to everything. How everything is connected to everything. Get it?"

The actors did seem to get it, finally. They went back to their encountering with gusto.

But in the audience, Waylon sighed. "I don't understand."

"What don't you understand, doll-face?" Marliana asked.

Waylon jerked a shoulder to the stage, where Neon was laughing at Baxter pretending to direct traffic. "Neon's play, or whatever she calls it. The whole thing seems nutty. I just don't get it."

Marliana pulled a tin from her tote bag, offered him a macaroon, then took one herself.

They ate together, savoring the sticky-crunchy deliciousness.

Marliana licked her fingers. "Neither do I," she admitted finally. "But it doesn't matter. Just look at her face."

Waylon helped himself to another macaroon and looked.

Since she'd turned fourteen last summer, Neon's face had seemed frozen in a permanent scowl. But now, aglow in the stage lights, there was his own sister Charlotte again, smiling the way she used to before that birthday.

"Look how happy it makes her to express herself!" Marliana whispered.

Waylon suddenly felt the need to explain his sister. "Neon's always been kind of weird. . . ."

"Oh no. She's not weird at all," Marliana

said. "She's wise. She knows how important it is to express one's passions."

"Not for me," Waylon muttered under his breath. He turned to the stage and set his jaw. No more talking about passions. He was a scientist. And scientists were strictly *im*passionate.

Two hours later, Neon released her cast members and walked Dumpster Eddy down the aisle.

When Marliana introduced herself, Neon closed her eyes. "Marliana Versala," she repeated, as if each syllable were a melted caramel. "What a wonderful name!"

Marliana lit up. "The most beautiful I could invent."

"Hold on," Waylon said. "You made it up?"

"It's a stage name, my dear. I chose it when I was fourteen years old. I knew then I was going to be an actress."

"I'm fourteen now!" Neon smacked her forehead at the coincidence. "And I made up a new name for myself. And I know what I'm going to be, too: a performance artist!"

"Of course you are, doll-face!" Marliana cheered. She offered Neon a macaroon and then toasted with one of her own. "Remember—your passion is your passion. It's *yours.* Stay true to it."

"I will," Neon promised solemnly.

"Don't ever let anyone tell you it isn't valuable."

"I never would, don't worry," Neon said. "And no one can talk me out of it, ever."

Waylon stood. All this talk about passions was making him antsy. "Let's go," he said, clipping on Eddy's leash. "All this talk about passions is making my dog antsy."

* * *

Neon surprised Waylon by asking to hold Eddy's leash on the way back to the station. Eddy pranced for her like the lead dog in an obedience class, squirrels suddenly the last thing on his mind.

At the station, she asked to feed Eddy his supper, and afterward, she hugged him good-bye.

She surprised Waylon once more as they started home. "I like your dog."

"And he sure liked you," Waylon answered. He felt half-jealous and half-proud of how Eddy had behaved.

Neon scuffed her boot along the sidewalk. "I wish he could live with us."

"He can't!" Waylon cried, louder than he'd meant to. He bit his lip against the soreness that swelled in his throat whenever he remembered that he could never take Eddy home, which was every single day.

"I *know* he can't," Neon said. "I was just *say-ing*. What's wrong with you?"

"Nothing's wrong with me! What's wrong with me is you need to change the subject. Oh, and also your clothes. You've got Eddy-hair on you now, and it could make Mom sick."

Neon stopped. She touched Waylon's arm.

"I'm sorry. I never realized how hard all this must be. What you have to go through to have that dog."

Waylon started walking again. He *really* needed to change the subject. "Hey, how come Mitchell wasn't there? You said you asked everyone in your class. Did he say no?"

Neon followed, scowling as if Waylon had just suggested she invite a bag of rotting garbage to be in her production. "Please. I didn't ask *him*."

"Why not? What's the matter with Mitchell?"

"Baseball is the matter with him."

"What's wrong with baseball?"

Neon shuddered. "Sports. So shallow. No art."

"Not the way Mitchell talks about it." Waylon considered this. "In fact, he sounds like you when he gets going about baseball, how

54

beautiful it is. It's his *passion*. And what about all that 'stay true to your passions, whatever they are' stuff back there?"

Neon narrowed her eyes, a finger to her chin. Waylon felt gratified that he'd used her own logic against her, and that she seemed to be considering it.

He opened his mouth to try to press his advantage, but his breath caught in his throat. He jumped behind a tree, flattened himself against the trunk, and motioned for Neon to join him. "Freeze," he ordered.

6

Waylon peered around the tree trunk. "That's the car I told you about. The one that brought Mom home yesterday," he whispered. "A guy with yellow hair was driving it." He stretched to peek over a branch and jumped back. "It's the same guy!"

Neon started to scoff, but then the passenger door opened and out stepped their mother. Just as she had on Thursday, she leaned into the window to say something to the two blond heads in the back.

This time, Waylon was close enough to make out the words. "Thanks, Oliver. Thanks, Maggie," his mother said. "See you tomorrow."

Then she waved good-bye and ran up the condo stairs smiling.

Waylon grabbed his sister's arm. "What do you think?"

"You sure that's the same car?" Neon asked. "Same guy, same kids?"

Waylon nodded. "Do you recognize him?" he asked hopefully. "Some work friend we don't know about?"

Neon shook her head. She stared up at the sixth floor, where their condo was. A frown deepened on her face.

"Have you looked at Dad lately?" she asked at last. "Those awful pajamas are probably stuck to him by now. He hasn't shaved in a week, and he doesn't smell so great, either. He barely comes out of his writing room, and when he does, he just grunts at us."

"So?" Waylon asked.

"So, who'd want a husband like that? You can't deny it—Dad's been a dud lately. Maybe she's interested in someone else."

"That's crazy! Besides, what about those kids?" Waylon thought back to the way his mom had tapped the little boy's nose. That was exactly what she used to do with him when he was little. "I don't think it's about Dad, Neon," Waylon said. "Or at least it's not *just* about him. I've been a dud, too. I've been spending every free minute with Eddy."

Neon's lower lip pooched out as she considered this. "I guess it's me, too," she admitted. "I've been practically living at the Rep. The way she patted that girl's hair—it was just how she used to pat mine."

Waylon took a step closer to his sister, and she took a step closer to him. They stood side by side for a long minute. Neon finally said the words Waylon was thinking. "Poor Mom. We've been a whole dud family. No wonder she wants to spend time with an upgraded version."

Waylon nodded. "Family Two-Point-Oh."

7

Waylon and Neon had tried all night long to get their mother to explain about that shiny blue car. She dodged every question and never cracked. After a while, their father had stuck his head out from his writing studio. "Leave her alone, kids," he'd said. "Everyone deserves a little privacy."

Waylon woke early Saturday, ready to try again.

From the kitchen, he heard his mother

singing as she folded laundry in the living room. Through the glass writing-room door, he saw his father already hunched over his keyboard, elbows flying. Waylon knocked and waved a thank-you for the platter of bacon on the counter.

Then he dropped two waffles into the toaster and sat down to plan his strategy.

Just then, Neon cruised in. "Rehearsal's at eleven. Bring that dog," she ordered.

"I will. Neon, maybe we should—"

She flapped her hands. "Shhh! Brainstorming. Got to create weather on the set today."

The waffles popped up, and she snatched them in midair.

"Nope," Waylon called. "Mine."

Neon stuck out her tongue. After she made a dramatic show of licking each waffle, she offered them back to him with an innocent smile. Waylon sighed and went to the freezer for two more. Neon shoved the waffles into her jacket pocket and floated out.

Mrs. Zakowski came in as Waylon was flooding his plate with syrup. Normally, she would have commented about breakfast not being a swimming event, but today she only took a bottle of mango juice from the fridge, humming.

"What's going on Thursday?" Waylon asked, choosing the direct attack. "How come you circled the date?"

Mrs. Zakowski put the bottle on the counter and gazed out the window over the sink. She tipped her head and smiled as if she was thinking about something nice.

A *secret* something nice.

It was the same smile, Waylon realized, she'd been wearing both times when she got out of the strange blue car. Waylon felt a little dizzy, as if the floor had just shifted. "Mom!"

"Oh! Oh, nothing much." She pulled a glass from the cupboard. "Say, I was thinking . . . there will probably be a cast party after Neon's performance. Maybe you'll be back from the Expo in time to celebrate, what do you think?"

"Mom. What's your circle for?"

Waylon's mother picked up the juice again. She filled her glass and then took her time screwing the cap back on the bottle. "Speaking of the Expo . . . there must be a lot of kids in this city getting pretty excited to meet Dr. Geller in person!"

Waylon sighed. Obviously he needed a new strategy.

He crowned his stack of waffles with bacon

and cut a wedge. "Maybe just me. I'm not sure anyone else has figured it out."

"Figured what out?"

"That she'll be there. I might be the only one." Waylon popped the waffle wedge into his mouth.

Mrs. Zakowski brought her juice to the table and sat down. "Hold on. You don't know for sure she'll be there?"

"I know, all right. See, her web page says she'll be lecturing at the library on the tenth. Then, on Friday, the fifteenth, she's doing a big presentation at the planetarium." He stabbed another piece of bacon and mopped it through the syrup, wishing for the millionth time that his dog could be under the table. Dogs love bacon.

"Uh . . . I'm missing something, buddy."

Waylon waved his fork in triumph. "Exactly.

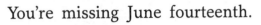

You're missing June fourteenth. The fourteenth is open on her web page. She's going to show up at the Science Expo, I just know it. Where else would she go?"

Mrs. Zakowski wagged a cautionary finger. "You're supporting your theory with inductive reasoning—your premises aren't certain facts. You know that isn't scientifically reliable."

Waylon shrugged. "I know, Mom, but . . . I can't explain it, but I'm positive I'm going to meet her. Maybe even show her my comic, *Cosmo-Quest.*"

"Well, I guess there's a pretty good chance you're right. We'd better get you a haircut this morning so you can look your best."

"Dr. Geller doesn't care about my—" Waylon stopped. He remembered the way his mother had smiled as she waved good-bye to the two kids in her new 2.0 family. "I mean *sure, Mom!* And let's hang out together after the haircut. It'd be great to spend some time with you!"

Waylon's mom frowned. She pressed the back of her hand to his forehead. "No fever," she mused.

"And Dad!" Waylon added. "He could get a haircut, too. He's really handsome when he gets a haircut, remember?"

Mrs. Zakowski tilted her head. She squinted as if she were trying to place the boy in front of her.

Then she shook her head. "Your dad could use a trim, that's for sure. But not today. He's submitting his screenplay to that big movie producer. Go get dressed. We can sneak in a haircut if we leave by nine."

Waylon left and hurried into his clothes.

As he dressed he worried. Had his mom really thought he might be sick, just because he said he wanted to spend some time with her? Or did she think that was funny?

While brushing his teeth, he worried about something else.

Obviously, Dr. Geller wanted her appearance at the Expo to be a surprise—why else wouldn't she announce it on her web page? So how would she feel if some kid didn't act surprised?

Disappointed, that's how. Waylon sure wasn't going to be the kid who disappointed Dr. Margaret J. Geller.

He needed to look surprised Thursday night.

Waylon spat out his toothpaste. He clapped his hands to his cheeks and made big Os of his eyes and mouth. Then he looked into the mirror.

And jumped back. He looked like that famous painting, the one with the skeleton-y

guy on the bridge, screaming as if someone was coming to murder him.

He tried again, a little smiley-er.

Now he looked like a clown, the kind that had terrified him when he was little.

He closed his eyes and imagined hard. Dr. Margaret J. Geller, one of the greatest scientists in Boston, standing right in front of him, admiring his display on sound waves. His heart skidded, and he felt his jaw fall slack. He opened his eyes. The kid in the mirror didn't look surprised, but he did look awestruck.

Awestruck would have to be good enough.

8

Waylon hurried to the police station straight from the barbershop. He made Eddy sit as usual while he worked his way into his jumpsuit. His neck was already scratchy from hair clippings, but he felt even itchier when he zipped up. The jumpsuit was hot.

It was only June. Summers in Boston got really steamy. He was going to broil playing with Eddy all summer in this thing. And speaking of hot summers—the Zakowskis always went to the beach for a week in August—how would he explain that to Eddy?

Waylon drove these worries out of his mind. He had a dog. That was the only thing that mattered. So what if things weren't perfect?

"Let's go," he said as he clipped on the leash. "Don't want to keep your new favorite person waiting."

Eddy seemed to understand. He trotted the whole way to the theater, dragging Waylon behind. When they got there, he dropped to the floor at Neon's heels, Mr. Obedience Class again. Waylon fell into a front-row seat right under the big fan, panting.

It seemed his sister had managed to talk a bunch more kids into joining the cast, and with Clementine there today, too, the stage looked pretty full. Neon attached the rolls of toilet paper to everybody, then explained the directions to the new kids. "My dad will act out a stage of life for two minutes, in the center-stage light, then the spotlight will go on you guys, and you'll do your encountering for five minutes. Show lots of emotion. It's called *emoting*."

The new kids got the idea right away, and the old bunch must have worked up some fresh acts overnight. Waylon saw groups of kids pretend to surf and climb trees and break dishes and paint one another's toenails, all with great drama.

And crash into one another. It had to be said—the stage was in chaos. Especially at the cornucopia steps, where knots of kids crawled over each other to slide down again and start new encounters.

Neon whistled for attention. She crouched, grabbed her head, and squeezed her eyes shut. "Quiet, quiet!" she cried. "Genius idea forming . . ."

Then she shot up, both fists in the air. "Of course! Half of you will enter through the audience. Crisscross the rows, so your toilet paper trails over them. This way, the audience is part of the abundance!"

Neon's voice rose and her cheeks flushed. "Yes, genius! Okay, kids with even-numbered birthdays, enter through the cornucopia. Odd, through the audience. Clementine, your job is to make sure things keep moving smoothly in the vomitorium, and Bax—"

"Wait a minute! Wait a minute!" Clementine flew headfirst out of the cornucopia. She made a face Waylon had never seen before on a human being: eyes rolling around, mouth working as if a toad had jumped in there and she had nowhere to spit it out. "Wait just a minute," she finally managed. "My job is *what*?"

"When the lights go down, station yourself

inside the vomitorium. It's narrow in there.
Make sure people keep moving."

"Neon, I don't think your play is so bad that
people are going to throw up." Clementine

crossed her arms over her chest. "But if they do, I'm definitely not cleaning it up."

"First of all, it's not a play, it's a *performance*." Neon sighed. "Second of all, a vomitorium is a hidden passageway in a theater. Performers can enter through it." She pointed to an arched opening Waylon hadn't noticed before, tucked under the balcony. "The odd-numbered-birthday kids will come pouring out of there, run down the aisles, and join up again on the stage. Get it?"

"Okay, fine," Clementine agreed grudgingly. "But just in case, leave some paper bags around. And lots of ginger ale. People really like ginger ale after they throw up."

Waylon caught Clementine's eye and shot her a thumbs-up. He really did like ginger ale after he vomited. Ginger ale was a fresh start for your mouth.

After rehearsal, Baxter offered to walk with Waylon and Eddy back to the station. "I'm having lunch with my dad. The cops get meatball subs on Saturdays," he said. "Hey, want to eat with us?"

Waylon shook his head, although he loved meatball subs and he was starving again. What he wanted to do was play with Eddy all afternoon, but he wasn't going to do that, either. He was going to try once more to find out the truth about his mom.

"What's the matter?" Baxter asked as soon as they left the Rep. "You look upset."

Baxter was a good detective. Waylon worked up an I'm-not-upset smile. But then it struck him again: Baxter *was* a good detective.

He dropped the smile. "Something's going on with my mom. She's been gone a lot lately. I've seen her getting out of a strange blue car twice now. There's a family inside. She says good-bye to the kids as if she's their mother. You got any ideas for how I could find out what she's doing?"

Baxter shrugged. "Ask her?"

Waylon shook his head. "I've tried. She gets a weird look on her face and changes the subject."

"A weird look? Is the weird look melty? If someone's in love, they get a melty look on their face."

Waylon remembered how gooey Marco had looked last year when he was in love with Lilly. Now, that was weird. Then he thought back to the expression on his mother's face as she had gazed out the window this morning. He shook off the memory. "No, not melty. More like she has a secret. I don't know. Maybe she just got a ride home those two times, and she doesn't even know them. How can I find out?"

"Hairs. Hairs are clues."

"Hairs?"

"People shed constantly. If your mom's doing mom things with that other family, their hairs are falling off on her. If she's just getting a ride home, they aren't. You should check her clothes."

Waylon didn't answer. The idea of snooping around his mother's clothes made him feel sick.

They walked in silence until they reached the station. On the steps, Baxter tapped his junior-officer badge. "I know! I can tail her. I'll wear a disguise, follow her from work, find out where she's going."

At that, Waylon felt like he might actually throw up. There wasn't enough ginger ale in the world to make him feel better now. He peeled off the jumpsuit and handed Eddy's leash to

Baxter. "You take him in, okay? I've got to go."

Once he was home, he positioned himself at the door and prepared some strategies to find out what the heck was going on with his mother.

It turned out, he didn't need any of them.

"Oh, my goodness," Mrs. Zakowski said, fanning her face as she walked in. "Summer's come early." She reached around Waylon and hung her sweater on a hook. "I'm going to take a nice cool shower." And then she left.

Waylon tried not to look. He really did. But there it was, in front of his nose: a dark purple sweater.

Covered with bright blond hairs.

"Neon," he yelled. "Get out here!"

9

___

"**M**y father's not the star of the show, because there is no star of the show, because *life* is the star of the show," Neon reminded her cast when Mr. Zakowski went to the dressing room to get in costume at Sunday's rehearsal. "His role is to represent the stages. Think of him like an hourglass, emptying right in front of us, reminding us that life is fleeting.

"No music, no weather today," Neon went on. "Just practice your acting around my dad.

Lots of emoting." Then she ordered everyone into position, dragged the velvet curtains closed, and called for her crew to cut the lights.

"Open the curtains and cue the center-stage spot!" she yelled when all was ready.

The curtains parted, and a bright circle of light snapped on. In the middle of the stage, rolled into a tight ball, was Waylon's father. He wore a pink leotard and a bald cap.

Nothing else.

He began to writhe and uncurl himself.

Waylon clapped his hands over his eyes, aghast. Then he peeked through his fingers.

His dad didn't have a lot of hair to begin with, but Waylon suddenly saw how important that hair was. He also realized how important clothes were, especially for a man who didn't spend much time—okay, *any* time—in a gym.

Because right now, Waylon's father looked an awful lot like a giant pink slug.

The giant slug made little mewing sounds, then rubbed his eyes as if the light hurt them.

He was being born, Waylon realized in horror.

Mercifully, the center-stage light cut away from Mr. Zakowski and swung over to the cornucopia. Kids tumbled out and wandered around, toilet paper streaming behind them. More kids spewed from the vomitorium, running down the aisles and scrambling onto the stage. Whenever someone passed him, the pink slug/baby gained another fluttering of toilet paper.

The cast had gotten more creative. Waylon watched pairs of kids cut down trees, board planes, and dance the hula. Whenever Anisha shined the red flashlight on an encounter, the actors added dialogue.

After a few minutes of spirited encountering, the spotlight moved again. Now Waylon's father was wearing a diaper over his leotard.

A giant diaper. Waylon's father was toddling around the stage in a giant diaper. He shook a pretend rattle, fell down, then set to wailing.

Waylon felt like wailing himself. It was by far the most embarrassing thing he had ever witnessed.

The cycles rolled on: five minutes of encountering by two dozen kids and one dog, then two minutes of Mr. Zakowski acting out a new stage of life.

The five-minute encountering parts were fine, but in his pink leotard Waylon's father hooted like a frantic chimpanzee at the child stage, muscled around as a teenager, and looked like he was about to melt when he rocked his own little baby.

At each new life stage, Waylon sank deeper and deeper into his seat.

When he reached the work stage of life, Waylon's dad yanked himself back and forth by an imaginary necktie, choking in anguish. With this stage, he reached his acting pinnacle.

Or maybe, Waylon wondered, maybe he wasn't acting.

Was this really how his father had felt at his old job? He had talked about that job as if it were choking him, and about that accounting office as if it were a prison.

Mr. Zakowski was going to have to return to that job if he didn't sell his screenplay. This thought was so terrible, Waylon lost track of what was happening onstage.

He snapped back to attention with a start when the spotlight moved again.

There stood his father, draped in yards of gray fabric that hung off him like elephant hide. In the saggy old-age skin, he crumpled to the stage floor and moaned creakily as death came for him, and the curtain fell.

Waylon breathed a huge sigh of relief and grabbed Eddy's leash from the floor. The whole humiliating performance was finally over.

Except it wasn't. "Hold on," Neon called from the wings. "Life is a circle, remember? New life from death. Center spot, please, and open the curtain."

And there, squirming around in his tight pink leotard, was the giant slug. Waylon's dad stretched his arms and began to squawk his newborn self into life again.

Waylon shot out of his seat, scooped Eddy off the stage, and bolted from the theater.

When Waylon got home after sharing a pizza with Eddy in the park, he found most of his family in the kitchen. "Where's Mom?" he asked.

Neon, who sat at the table covering cardboard stars and lightning bolts with aluminum foil, pointed her scissors at a note. "Says she'll be home at dinnertime."

Waylon exchanged a worried look with his sister.

Mr. Zakowski walked by, head down, hands clasped behind his

back. He circled the kitchen, made a quick circuit around the living room, paced into his writing room and back out again.

Waylon hopped onto the counter to watch. "No word yet," he guessed when his father emerged again.

"Too soon. Probably not until tomorrow, my agent thinks." Mr. Zakowski paced between the refrigerator and the stove three times. "I'm going crazy."

"Why don't you cook something?" Waylon suggested. "That always helps when you're waiting to hear back."

Mr. Zakowski snapped his fingers. "Of course. But what?"

For a second, Waylon thought about the boxes of butterscotch pudding in the cupboard. He was suddenly starving again, and butter-scotch pudding was one of those rare foods that really delivered. It tasted as good as it smelled, it smelled as good as it looked, and it looked as good as it felt in your mouth. Butterscotch pudding even sounded good—you could slurp it in a satisfying way.

But then he had a better idea. "How about a cake? Mom's favorite is red velvet."

"I know," Mr. Zakowski said. "I've forgiven her for that."

"What do you mean, forgiven?"

"Red velvet isn't a flavor. Red velvet cake is just a cake with fake coloring in it. Now, chocolate is a flavor, coconut is a flavor. Carrot is a flavor. How about a carrot cake?" He pulled down a cookbook and started flipping through the pages.

Waylon cast a glance at Neon. Neon looked up for a second and nodded. "But *Mom* loves red velvet," he said. "We should do something nice for *her*."

Mr. Zakowski flung his arms over his head as if he were being attacked by vampires. "It isn't even a real thing! Some salesman invented it to sell more food dye. Red velvet is an abomination—no real chef will make it."

Neon slammed the box of foil on the table. She pointed a lightning bolt at her father. "Red velvet," she said firmly. "With hearts on top." Then she stuffed the silvery props into a garbage bag and headed back to the Rep.

Mr. Zakowski sighed dramatically, but he began assembling ingredients. Waylon relaxed.

As he mixed the batter, Mr. Zakowski began to whimper.

"What's the matter?" Waylon asked, alarmed.

"Nothing. Just running my lines."

"Oh. For Neon's thing? But you don't have any lines."

"Okay, rehearsing, then." He threw his head back and wailed his being-born cry.

Waylon clapped his hands over his ears. "How can you do this, Dad? Aren't you embarrassed?"

Mr. Zakowski shrugged. "It's just acting." He let out a toddler shriek as he beat the eggs. Then he turned to face Waylon. "Besides, this is a really stressful time for me. Letting it out feels *good*. You should try it."

Waylon slid off the counter. "No thanks. It's time for my baseball lesson with Mitchell. Don't forget about the hearts on top of Mom's cake." He grabbed his mitt and hurried out.

10

Waylon sprang Eddy from the police station and headed over to the alley behind Mitchell's place. When they got there, Eddy went extra crazy, as usual. This was because, back in January, Waylon and Baxter had built him a dog igloo in this exact spot. Eddy had graduated from being a stray to being a respectable dog with his own boy and a collar and a license the week of the dogloo. Good times. Eddy remembered all this.

Of course, Eddy also went crazy because

there was a Dumpster out here, and Dumpster Eddy sure loved Dumpsters. He jumped up and gave a hopeful sniff at the lid.

"Nope, sorry, boy. That's in your past." Waylon hopped up and sat firmly on the lid to wait.

For a year now, Waylon had been helping Mitchell improve his already awesome baseball skills by teaching him the physics of the sport. In return, Mitchell had been trying to help Waylon actually play it.

Waylon loved the time he spent with Mitchell, but more and more, he realized he didn't love baseball. The problem was, Waylon couldn't figure out the point to any of it. "But I'm already *at* home plate," he'd remind Mitchell, over and over. "Why should I try to get around all those other bases to get home if I'm already *here*?"

Mitchell would just shake his head and aim another pitch at Waylon's bat. Somehow

Waylon's bat would manage to not be there when the ball arrived. Possibly because Waylon couldn't help jumping back when he saw the ball whizzing right for him.

By the time Mitchell came whistling around the corner, Waylon was thoroughly dejected. "Maybe I should try another sport, Mitchell," he said. "What about football? Think I'd be better at football?"

"Football? You, Science Dude?" Mitchell said. "I gotta be honest. Football is a bunch of really big guys knocking each other around. Stick with baseball. Baseball's beautiful." Then he surprised Waylon by grabbing his mitt from him and stuffing it into his own back pocket. "But we're not practicing today," he said. "I need you to help me with something. Let's go."

Waylon and Eddy followed as Mitchell trotted into his building. Mitchell dragged them into the elevator, up to the fifth floor, then into his apartment and down the hall to his bedroom.

"Better shut the door," Mitchell said. "My sister's cat hates dogs."

Waylon closed the door, and right away a cat started yowling in the hall. Eddy lay down at the door, smiling as if he was proud of what he'd caused.

Mitchell pointed to a big doughnut-shaped heap of cardboard and balsa wood on the center of the rug.

Waylon crouched for a closer look. The mess was painted a dozen shades of green. Every available surface was plastered with magazine clippings of crowds or markered with the names of gas stations and fast-food chains. A square of green carpet, crisscrossed with sandpaper, was tacked to the center of the pile. "Yikes, this is a total wreck," he said.

Mitchell leaped in front of the heap. "Science Dude! Some respect! This is a scale model of Fenway Park, the greatest baseball stadium ever built in the world."

"This? But it's all peeling and crooked. Look at this. . . ." He pointed to a wide piece of cardboard looming out of the corner at a disturbing angle.

"Science Dude! Respect!" Mitchell gasped again. "That is the Green Monster. That wall has won and lost World Series. That wall has built and crushed careers. That wall is legend."

"Well . . . if it's so great, what do you need me for?"

Mitchell leaned back against his bureau, a smug smile spreading over his face. "In December, I made this baby for my history project. Last month, I submitted it as my art project. And now, with your help, I'll turn it in as my science project, too. You tell me the science of this thing, and I'll write it down."

For the next hour, Mitchell scribbled notes as Waylon explained the principles of ball-field physics. At each topic—the frictional coefficient of walls, the projectile trajectory of home runs, the bounce velocity of natural turf—Mitchell's grin grew wider.

Lastly, Waylon got to the effect of gravity on everyday events. "According to my theory, if a batter waits for a plane to pass overhead before swinging, the plane's mass could counteract the Earth's gravity just a tiny bit, giving him an edge." At that, Mitchell actually hugged him.

"I should go," Waylon said. "I need to take Eddy back, then get home for dinner. We can do more tomorrow, or next week."

"Nah, I've got enough. Plus, it's due tomorrow. Thanks, Science Dude."

"Tomorrow?"

Mitchell shrugged as if waiting until the last minute for a science project was no big deal.

But walking to the station, Waylon wondered. For months, he'd spent all his free time working on his science project. And avoiding sports practice until the last minute. Mitchell had done the opposite. If Science and Sports were land masses on a planet, he and Mitchell were antipodes.

11

Mrs. Zakowski always left early on Mondays to get the lab ready for the week's work. This gave Waylon and Neon time to work on their dad at breakfast.

"Look what I found in your closet, Dad." Waylon pulled a crisp blue shirt, still in its dry-cleaning bag, from behind his chair.

"Mmm . . . this shampoo sure smells great!" Neon set the bottle in front of their dad's eggs with a firm thud. She added some shaving cream and a razor. "And look! There are instructions on the can, in case you forgot how to shave!"

"Very funny," Mr. Zakowski said. "I get the message."

Waylon plucked a cookbook from the shelf and flipped to the cookie section. "Mom loves cookies. Chocolate chip is her favorite."

"Nope, she likes peanut butter," Neon disagreed.

"Chocolate chip."

"Peanut butter."

Mr. Zakowski raised his coffee mug. "Peanut-butter-chocolate-chip cookies it is! And then I'll get myself spiffed up. See you tonight, kids."

All during school, Waylon found himself dreaming about chocolate-chip-peanut-butter cookies. He was thinking about them when he got to Neon's rehearsal, too, even though he'd eaten an extra sandwich at lunch. He settled into a seat to watch the show, trying to clear his mind.

Eddy was great that day, obeying every command, never getting distracted, even by the weather effects, which Waylon had to admit were pretty cool. A ceiling fan blew tinsel for rain and feathers for snow over the actors; turned up high, it created a cornmeal sand-storm.

"We'll rehearse with the coatrack all week," Neon announced to her cast. "That way, the performance will be fresh when my dad is back on Thursday night."

Seeing the coatrack in the center of the stage again made Waylon very happy. The coatrack was a whole lot less embarrassing than his father, who was back in the kitchen baking up something nice for his family.

Which reminded him of those cookies again.

As soon as rehearsal was over, Waylon hurried Eddy back and rushed home, practically drooling.

But when he got there, he smelled burned cookies from the hallway. Inside, cookie sheets covered with charred black lumps lined the counter.

Neon, flattened to the wall beside the fridge, was peeking through the doorway into the living room. She put a finger to her lips and waved for Waylon to join her.

Waylon dropped his backpack softly and peered around her shoulder.

Their dad sat slumped on the couch, his face planted in his hands. Their mom sat beside him.

Romantic? Waylon mouthed.

Opposite of romantic, Neon mouthed back.

Mrs. Zakowski patted her husband's back. "Can you tell me what's wrong?"

Mr. Zakowski didn't look up. "My agent called."

"Oh, dear. The producer didn't want it after all?"

"No, no, he does," Mr. Zakowski mumbled through his fingers. "In fact, he says it's exactly the kind of project he's been looking for. He wants to fly me out to Hollywood to discuss it."

When their mom lifted their dad's face toward her, Neon and Waylon raised hopeful eyebrows at each other. This did have romantic potential. "Well, that's wonderful," Mrs. Zakowski said. "Why so sad?"

"He's leaving Friday for three months of filming in Morocco," Mr. Zakowski said. "The only day he can meet with me is . . . Thursday. The fourteenth."

At that, Neon exploded off the wall and ran into the living room. "*Nooooooo!* You promised! The whole show—"

Mr. Zakowski lifted his palms. "I know. I know."

"You *have* to be in my performance, Dad!" Neon cried. "You're the center of the whole thing."

"I know, Charlotte."

"There's no one else who can do it."

"I know."

Neon stood in front of their father, quaking in fury.

Waylon began to shake also. Inside.

Because there was. There was one person who had sat through every rehearsal with the coatrack. One person who had watched Mr. Zakowski perform the role and who wasn't already in the production.

One person in the entire world.

And sooner or later, his family was going to figure out who that person was.

Waylon saw his father realize it first. A spark of hope flickered in his eyes. And then died.

Waylon's mother realized it next. She looked over at Waylon for a nanosecond. Then her whole body slumped. She shook her head at her husband. *Nope, not doing that to him,* her look said.

Nope, Mr. Zakowski's look agreed. *We are not even asking.*

And then it dawned on Neon.

She drew a deep breath. She lowered her head toward Waylon and turned on the Glare.

"I . . . but . . . no . . ." Waylon stumbled. "Dr. Margaret J. . . ."

Mr. Zakowski stood up. He put a hand on Neon's shoulder. "No," he said. "He's not giving up the Science Expo. I will do the performance." Two years of dreams were dying a horrible death on his face.

Waylon ran into his room, slammed the door, and flung himself onto his bed.

After a minute, he pulled *Biographies of Science Pioneers* from under the pillow. Reading about the trials of his heroes never failed to comfort him.

He opened the book and started to read. But tonight the familiar stories just made him feel worse.

Not a single pioneer had been asked to give up meeting a famous astrophysicist in order to go yowling around a stage in a pink leotard and a bald wig.

It wasn't fair. He was representing his school next Thursday night, the youngest student to do that, ever. And now he felt lousy about it.

He tossed the book on the floor and dove under the pillow. Thursday was ruined.

12

The look Neon leveled at Waylon when he came into the kitchen Tuesday morning was beyond anything she'd ever dished out before.

Waylon knew of an underground coal fire in Australia that had been burning for six thousand years. Neon's glare looked like it had been cooking a whole lot longer and hotter. His skin started to crisp under its fury.

He turned away and headed for his father's

writing room. But what he saw through the glass door stopped him cold.

Mr. Zakowski sat at his desk in front of a dark monitor. His whole body looked defeated. His shoulders slumped as if they could no longer hang on to his neck, and his hands hung limp by the floor, as if they didn't have the will to rise over the keyboard ever again. Even his bald spot seemed sad.

Waylon shouldered his backpack and left without looking back.

At school, he kept his head in his books. But the pages blurred and all he could see was the back of his father's head. At the board, Mrs. Fernman was talking, but all he could hear was his sister's ear-scorching silence.

After lunch, he asked for permission to take recess in the science room. "To make sure I'm ready for the Expo."

That wasn't true. He'd been ready for the Expo for months. But he needed to get away, and the science room felt like a second home.

First he stopped to say hello to his rat. Last year, he and Clementine had experimented with maze-learning on a rat named Eighteen. Eighteen had gotten lost for a while, and when they'd found her, she'd had babies. His science teacher had let Waylon adopt one of them— Eighteen and Three-Fifths—and he'd been teaching him tricks.

"Shake hands, Eighteen and Three-Fifths," Waylon asked, and the rat stretched up on his hind legs and extended a paw through the cage. Waylon shook it. "Wish me luck Thursday."

Mrs. Resnick came up beside him and handed him a bag of rat food. "You must be so excited."

Waylon shook a little food into Eighteen and

Three-Fifths's cup. For a moment, he thought about telling Mrs. Resnick what had happened last night—the whole messy situation with his sister's performance.

His science teacher would understand. She'd be on his side. She'd probably be outraged for him. *How unfair,* she'd probably say. *How could your sister expect such a ridiculous thing?*

But Mrs. Resnick was almost as excited about

the Expo as he was. If he told her, the night would be ruined for her the way it was ruined for him. "I can't wait," he told her instead. "I'm going to be a scientist when I grow up, and—"

"You already are," Mrs. Resnick reminded him.

Waylon smiled. "And Thursday night, I'll meet so many of them. Lots of scientists will probably come, don't you think? Maybe they'll let me visit their labs. Maybe I could watch their experiments. Maybe I could even help them!"

Waylon didn't mention the one scientist he really hoped would come Thursday. Meeting Dr. Geller felt too private, too thrilling a hope to share.

"Absolutely," Mrs. Resnick agreed. "Quite an opportunity. Boston's full of universities and labs. Scientists will come from all over, maybe farther away than just Boston. And the science teachers in the whole school district—we'll all be there. We're so proud of you."

"What if I mess up?"

"You won't." She motioned to the lumpy shape under the protective shower curtain. "It's a fine project, Waylon. It's clear, well researched, and interesting. And I know you. I know that whatever happens Thursday night, you will make us proud."

Waylon went back to his classroom feeling better. But when the dismissal bell rang, he realized he had a new problem.

Baxter was going to take Eddy to the rehearsal. His friends, his sister, even his dog would be at the Rep this afternoon, where he couldn't show his face. And he sure didn't want to go home and risk looking at how sad his father was.

That meant there was no place he could go, nobody to spend time with.

Wait. There was still one place and one person. . . .

Waylon took off. As he reached the alley, he saw Mitchell behind his building, clutching his bat as if it were his only friend.

Even from a distance, Waylon saw that tears shimmered in his eyes. Tears. In the eyes of the greatest baseball superstar Boston Little League had ever known. "What's wrong?" he called, running toward his friend.

Mitchell wiped his face and spun away.

Waylon stopped a few respectful feet back. "Crying's natural, you know," he offered, remembering the information in *The Science of Being Human,* Chapter Seven, "People Plumbing" that often made him feel better.

"I know that," Mitchell said without turning

around. "Carl Yastrzemski cried when they retired his number. David Ortiz, at his five hundredth home run. Lou Gehrig, when he left baseball." Mitchell's shoulders shook.

"So it's baseball? Something happened in baseball?"

Mitchell pulled a crumpled piece of paper from his pocket. He handed it over.

Waylon read the note. He sighed. "It's just a bad grade, Mitchell. I was worried it was

something terrible, like you couldn't play base-ball anymore."

Mitchell finally turned around then. "It *is* that, Science Dude!" he wailed. "It's that exactly!" He took the note back and shook it. "I had a D in Science going in. That Fenway Park project was my only hope of raising my grade enough to pass, and look—he's giving me two Fs. One F for the project, and one F for present-ing it."

"How come? Didn't he like it?"

Mitchell buried his face in his hands. "He did. Until . . ."

"Until what?"

"Yoga class."

"Yoga class?"

"And smoothies."

Waylon grabbed Mitchell's arm. *"Explain."*

Mitchell gulped in a steadying breath. "My

science teacher is in a yoga class with my history teacher. Apparently they went out for smoothies after class last night at a place near Fenway Park. My science teacher said, 'Oh, Fenway Park. That reminds me . . .' and he told her about my project. 'Hmm . . . Fenway Park,' my history teacher said. 'That sure sounds a lot like his history project.' So: busted."

"Oh. Sorry. But still . . . it's only a grade," Waylon tried.

Mitchell raised his gaze to Waylon's. "It *isn't* only a grade. If I don't pass science, I don't pass eighth grade. If I don't pass eighth grade, I—"

"Don't get into ninth grade," Waylon said. "I get it."

"No, you *don't* get it! It's *way* more important. If I don't pass eighth grade, I have to go to summer school. Which means I can't play summer baseball. So I have to pass eighth grade, Science Dude! I *have* to!"

"I'm really sorry," Waylon said. "Maybe summer school won't be—" And then it struck him. "Did you say you'd get a full grade for presenting a science project?"

Mitchell nodded miserably. "You know anybody who needs a science project presented?"

Waylon had a sudden vision. His dreams—the ones he'd shared with Mrs. Resnick today and the one that was too private to share—were stacked up gloriously high, like a skyscraper. And then the skyscraper imploded in slow motion, story by story, until all that was left was a cloud of dust.

Waylon shook his head to clear the image. He took a steadying breath. "Unfortunately, I do."

13

Wednesday afternoon, Waylon waited in anguish outside the junior high doors. *Please let Mitchell's teacher say no,* he prayed with every breath. When Mitchell finally showed up, Waylon braced himself and walked over. "My teacher said okay. How about yours?"

Mitchell grinned and gave two thumbs up. "We're on, Science Dude," he said.

And Waylon's heart crashed.

He forced himself to picture his father, with

the sad bald spot, sitting in front of the blank screen. "That's great!" he said in the most convincing voice he could muster. "Now, let's get going. I have a lot to teach you in twenty-four hours. We just have to make one stop first."

At the theater, Waylon found his dad tinkering with some speakers. He explained everything quickly, hoping his voice wouldn't waver.

When he was finished, his father stared at him for a very long time. "Are you sure, son?" he said at last.

Waylon wasn't. Not at all. But he'd seen hope bloom again on his father's face. "I'm sure," he said.

Before he could change his mind, he crossed the stage to where his sister had her head poked up inside the cornucopia. He tapped her shoulder.

Neon's head emerged. Her eyes bugged out in disbelief: *How dare her failure of a brother show his face?*

"Mitchell's going to present my project so I can do the part so Dad can go to Hollywood," he explained before she could explode.

Neon twisted away with a disbelieving sneer.

Waylon took her arm and turned her back. "Really. I'll do it. Take Dad's part."

Neon tossed her thumb toward Mitchell. "*He's* going to present your project?"

"Yeah! So now I can take Dad's part, Neon."

"Him??? The *jock* is going to present a *science* project?"

"Yes, Neon. Did you hear me? Dad can meet with that movie guy. I can do his part now. Did you even hear me?"

Probably Neon hadn't. There seemed to

be steam coming out her ears. Her head was lowered and she was actually pawing the floorboards like a cartoon bull, about to gore some poor clown.

And then, just as it struck Waylon who that poor clown was, she charged. Waylon flailed his arms in wild warning at Mitchell.

Mitchell stood frozen, eyes saucered like a deer's in oncoming headlights, as Neon barreled toward him.

Every kid in the theater turned to watch.

Neon skidded to a halt at Mitchell's feet. She grabbed his head by the ears and yanked it down to hers.

And planted a loud kiss right on his mouth.

The auditorium went dead silent.

Neon turned back to face her brother. She lowered her head again.

Before she could charge and plant one on him, too, Waylon grabbed his backpack and tore out of the building.

Waylon had a hard time getting his pupil to concentrate at first. Mitchell hadn't said a word on the way to his place, and he didn't say anything when they got inside. He flopped down on his rug and stared at the ceiling.

"Sounds are waves of vibrations moving through a medium—air, usually," Waylon began the lesson. "They cause our eardrums to vibrate."

There was no response, but Waylon went on. "No medium means no sound. Like in space—there's no atmosphere, so no one would hear you if you screamed."

Still no response, but Waylon carried on—through transverse and longitudinal waves, through compressions and echoes. Every once in a while, Mitchell rolled over and gave Waylon a worried look. "Am I bleeding?" he asked, his fingers brushing his lips. "Did she leave a mark?"

Waylon assured Mitchell that Neon hadn't scarred him and then went back to the lesson. But it was clear the information wasn't sinking in, until he happened upon a successful strategy.

"There sure are a lot of sounds at a baseball

game," Waylon said, hanging the words in the air like bait.

Mitchell sat up. "You mean when I hit a line drive, that *crack!* is just vibrations?" he asked.

"Right. The sound waves originate when your bat collides with the ball. All sound—"

"Which is a *really hard* collision," Mitchell pointed out. "My bat's on fire this year."

"Yes, and all the other sounds, too. Like"— Waylon paused to come up with a baseball sound—"like a fielder catching the ball in his glove."

"Not from that liner I just hit," Mitchell said. "No fielder could get anywhere near that rocket."

"Okay then, let's imagine the crowd, cheering for you. Think of all those larynges, sending all those cheer vibrations out into the ball field,

which amplifies the sound waves because it contains them, like a drum."

"Whoa, right!" Mitchell cried. "It was probably a triple I hit. I probably drove in a couple of runs, won the game. Hey, maybe I should bring my Fenway model to help people get it," he offered.

"No thanks," said Waylon, gathering up his

backpack. "We'd better use my display. I'll show you how it works tomorrow at the Expo."

Leaving Mitchell's building, Waylon ran into Clementine coming home from the rehearsal.

"Hey," she said. "So now that your sister kissed Mitchell, does that make him your boyfriend-in-law?"

"No. What? Of course not," Waylon sputtered.

"Because," Clementine continued, "you should be boyfriend and girlfriend with Margaret now. Margaret is Mitchell's sister, so—"

Waylon never heard the rest of her reasoning. He was halfway home before the lobby doors slammed behind him.

14

Thursday morning, Waylon woke up so early the sky was deep violet and still sprinkled with stars. He heard hushed voices coming from the kitchen.

"The cab will be here any minute," his mom said. "You can't be late."

"Just this one last thing," said Waylon's dad.

And then footsteps tiptoed down the hall. Waylon's door opened.

"Oh, you're awake," his dad whispered. He

came in and sat on the bed. He held out a folded note. "I was going to leave this."

Waylon put the note on the night table, on top of *Biographies of Science Pioneers*. "Good luck today, Dad," he said. And he meant it. Still, before the words were out of his mouth, he felt a ball of dread gather in his stomach.

"To you, too, buddy. That's what I said in the note. I'm so proud of what you're doing—"

Waylon put up a hand. He rolled away. What he was doing tonight was giving him a stomachache.

"Okay, okay," his dad said quietly. "Close your eyes. Get some sleep." And then he left the room.

Waylon closed his eyes. But he didn't get any sleep.

* * *

School on Thursday was excruciating.

All day long, Waylon was consumed with images: The pink leotard. The bald wig. The wailing and moaning.

On the playground, he flung himself onto the blacktop, wondering if he could get out of the performance if he broke his face. Probably not. Neon would just say broken faces were a vital part of *The Everything*.

The one good thing, he kept reminding himself, was that outside of the kids who were actually in the performance, nobody he knew was going to see it. The parents of the cast members would come, and so would some of the Rep regulars, but otherwise, Neon said, they hadn't sold a lot of tickets.

Clementine came running up. "I asked Margaret," she panted, pulling up her socks.

"She said okay. . . . Why are you lying on the blacktop? Are you having a heart attack?"

Waylon lifted his chin an inch. "I might be. You asked Margaret what?"

"About being your girlfriend. She says you can buy her a ring."

He scrambled to his feet. "What? No! Margaret wants me to be her *boyfriend*?"

"Not at first she didn't, of course," Clementine

said. "But when I reminded her you were going to invent all these great things, she said okay. She wants you to start with an antibacterial lipstick. For when you try to kiss her."

"But I don't want a girlfriend. I especially don't want *that* girlfriend! And I'm sure not going to kiss her!" Waylon grabbed his hair and tugged, making room for the headache that had sprung up. The day couldn't get any worse.

Except then it did.

"Well, maybe this will make you feel better," Clementine said. "I told Principal Rice about the show."

"What? You told her about *The Everything?*" Waylon gasped. "Why did you do that? She might come!"

"Well, sure. That's the point. Now at least we'll have one nice person in the audience. Plus, maybe we'll finally get to see her husband."

"Her husband?"

"She's a *Mrs.*, so that means there's a Mr. Rice. I've been wondering about him my whole life."

"Oh, great. So now I'll have to worry about Mrs. Rice *and* her husband seeing me in that stupid pink leotard."

Clementine cocked her head. "You mean your fake-naked costume? That's not stupid."

Waylon startled. "Excuse me? My *what* costume?"

Clementine shrugged. "Fake-naked. That's what Neon called it. She explained that it represents human vulnerability throughout life. Except of course when you're a helpless baby, and your parents protect you a little. That's represented by the diaper."

Waylon grabbed his stomach. "I can't do this," he groaned. "It's going to be horrible."

"What are you so worried about?" Clementine asked. "We're the ones doing all the work. You just have to stand there."

"What do you mean?"

Clementine straightened up tall and held her arms out rigid. "We've been rehearsing all week with that coatrack. It went great. All you have to do is act as well as a coatrack."

Just then, the Recess-Is-Over bell rang. Clementine skipped into the building and Waylon staggered along behind.

Inside, he propped up his geography book and slumped down behind it. Facing him was a picture of an arctic tundra. They had studied this chapter back in September. Back when his life was simple. But his life had also been barren, like this tundra, Waylon realized. He hadn't met Dumpster Eddy back then.

He flipped to the last chapter, "Jungle

Ecosystems." Jungle ecosystems were complicated, like his life had become. Now he had his mother's mystery to worry about. And a girlfriend he didn't want. Worst of all, he was facing a humiliating performance instead of the Science Expo.

But maybe Clementine was right—maybe he just had to stand there. Of course, Mrs. Rice seeing him fake-naked was definitely a bad development. But Mrs. Rice was retiring this year—after next week, he'd never see her again.

By the time the intercom crackled for the end-of-school announcements, he felt a little better. Mrs. Rice keyed a fake drumroll and congratulated the birthday kids and reminded everyone to check the lost-and-found before school ended next week.

Then, instead of sounding the dismissal buzzer, she played the fake drumroll again and cleared her throat. "And finally, a special announcement," she boomed. "Tonight at seven there will be a production of *The Everything* at the Beantown Rep. It was written by one of our own alumni, Miss Charlotte Zakowski, and stars several of your classmates. I've called the theater and learned there are still plenty of tickets available. Let's show some school spirit and fill that auditorium!"

15

Starting off to the Expo Center, Waylon's project safely wedged between him and Mitchell in the backseat, Mrs. Zakowski couldn't stop telling them both how proud she was of what they were doing. Mitchell answered her, but Waylon didn't. Every time she mentioned Neon's performance, he felt sicker.

At last she gave up, and for a minute Waylon was relieved. But then she started a happy humming, and he felt even worse.

Which was confusing. He loved his mom, so he wanted her to be happy, of course. But something about her humming today made him feel worried. He only wanted his mom to be happy if his family was the one making her happy. Not some other family.

"Can you put the radio on, Mom?" he said.

Mitchell shot Waylon a funny look. Waylon turned and pressed his forehead against the glass for the rest of the way.

The Expo Center was huge, with soaring ceilings. Excitement buzzed in the air along with the fluorescent lights and the voices of a hundred nervous kids.

Waylon focused on setting up his display. Mitchell followed along as Waylon showed him how to use each piece: the Slinky, the drum, the water balloons people could press to their

ears. "If you don't know something, just point to the display," Waylon wrapped up when he was pretty sure Mitchell understood. "What really matters tonight is—"

"I know, Science Dude. You've told me a thousand times. What matters is when this Dr. Geller person comes by."

"Exactly." Waylon pulled out the picture he carried in his wallet and showed it to Mitchell. "When you see this woman, don't act all fanboy, but don't act too bored, either. Be cool, but not too cool. Got it?"

"I've got it, don't worry."

"And remember to tell her you're not me! And that—"

"And that she can email you or call you up, or whatever, anytime. And that sure, you could help her discover galaxies and things. I *know*."

"Okay. But remember, don't be too—"

"Science Dude!" Mitchell covered his ears and reeled back. "Your sound waves are killing me! Stop already! I know what to do—tell this Geller lady how much you want to be a baseball player when you grow up—"

"That's not funny, Mitchell." Waylon slid the picture back into his wallet, careful not to wrinkle the edges.

"Yes it is. In fact, it's hilarious—you should have seen your face." Mitchell took the Red Sox cap off his head and tugged it down over Waylon's. "Listen. This thing you're doing is awesome. You're helping me with my science grade, and you're also helping your sister with her performance and your father with selling his screenplay. That's a triple play—three outs in the same play—which is so rare it's only happened

seven hundred and ten times in the whole history of professional baseball. That is *awesome*."

A triple play. Waylon hadn't thought about it that way. "Really?" he asked.

"Actually, wait, no. It's even more awesome than that. It's an *unassisted* triple play. That's so rare it's only happened fifteen times."

"Unassisted?"

"That's where the same player makes all three outs. That's you. You're doing it by yourself. So get out of here and start doing it."

Waylon tugged the cap down tight, hoping it would keep this encouraging thought in his head, then ran to the waiting car.

The Red Sox cap did not work. Every inch of the drive to the Rep seemed an hour of agony, and yet in what felt like a matter of seconds, they were at the back door.

Waylon looked over at his mother. For the briefest second he thought about begging for help. *Don't make me do this, Mom*—the words actually formed in his throat.

But those days were over. He wasn't a little boy anymore, and she couldn't make the bad things go away.

"I'm hungry," he said instead.

"I know that," she said back. She took one hand off the wheel and pushed over her pocketbook. "Three granola bars in there. I'll bring ham sandwiches to the cast party."

Waylon peeled open the three granola bars and ate them, one after the other, his head slumped against the window.

And then it was time.

"It's only thirty-five minutes of your life," his mother said, as if she were inside his head with him. "And the spotlight's only on you seven times. For what? About fourteen minutes?"

"I know that," he said. And then he got out of the car.

Neon led Waylon to the dressing room, blathering on about emoting the whole way. "Six stages. Obviously, start with birth and end with death, then repeat birth. You don't need to do what Dad did in between. You can improvise. Just emote a lot."

Waylon bit his lip and pictured the coatrack. How much emoting would Neon have gotten out of that coatrack?

When they got to the dressing room, he was surprised for a minute to find no one inside.

And then he remembered.

He was the only one with a costume. Everyone else would be wearing their regular clothes. "Why can't I wear my regular clothes?" he asked. "Why do I have to be fake-naked?"

Neon shook her head. She pointed to a neat pile on the dressing table. "Put on the pink leotard now. And the bald cap. You never take those off," she said. "Practice putting on the diaper and the gray skin, make sure you can do it right. Bring them onstage with you, leave them at your feet."

Waylon lifted the adult diaper and the hideous gray skin and held them out, pinched between his fingertips. Words failed him. He looked at his sister, begging her to understand.

"Don't worry, little brother. Everything is going to be all right," Neon said in a surprisingly consoling voice. "The stage is above the audience's eye level, so nobody will see the pile at your feet."

That was not what Waylon had been worried about.

Neon tapped the clock beside the door as she left. "Ten minutes to curtain," she said brightly.

16

Waylon stood in the center of the wooden stage floor, looking down.

Seeing his bare feet was a surprising comfort. When you are wearing a pink leotard and a bald wig, it is nice to see something familiar, like your feet.

You can do this, his feet seemed to be saying. And he could. Thirty-five minutes, that was all. He could be as good as a coatrack for thirty-five minutes.

"Cue music!" Neon's voice hissed through the drawn curtains in front of him.

Neon had slashed open a washing-machine carton to make a hiding spot just below the stage. When she was in place, the audience would only see a sheet of cardboard that read MAYTAG—CLEANING POWER YOU TRUST. But when the curtains opened, anyone onstage could see her, and she could see them.

Waylon heard her hiss again. "Thirty seconds!"

He curled himself into a ball.

And the velvet curtains swept open.

Waylon heard the center spotlight snap on and felt it burn hot on his back. He rose on stiff coatrack legs and spread his coatrack arms.

And held still. With the spotlight on him, Waylon couldn't see the audience, but after a while, he could hear them shuffling around in their seats. A few cleared their throats. A few more coughed impatiently.

The coatrack did not care.

Neon would care, of course. Waylon would have to endure her wrath for a good long time, he figured. He might have to remain a not-caring coatrack forever.

At last the other two dozen kids were cued to come pouring onto the stage, half from the cornucopia, half from the audience. They began joyfully encountering, weaving their toilet paper trails around him.

Everything, Waylon was surprised to see, went just as it was supposed to go. There were no collisions, no one got stuck in the cornucopia, and the tinsel rain fell in convincing showers. Whenever the actors saw the red flashlight on them, they rose to the occasion with sparkling bits of conversation.

Waylon began to enjoy the show. But then he heard Neon hiss his name. He looked over the stage rim.

Neon pointed to the diaper at his feet, tapping her timer. The five minutes were up.

She made a threatening gesture.

Waylon stepped into the diaper and began to pull it up.

And then Neon stuck out her tongue.

The coatrack in the halfway-up diaper tried to hold still. But Waylon was angry now. And it struck him: if there was ever a time to let it out, that time was now. *It's just acting,* his dad had said. *It feels good.*

Waylon raised his arms and stomped his feet in full-fledged waffle outrage.

Neon's eyes popped in shock. And then she tipped her head. She nodded and began to silently applaud.

Waylon realized she thought he was emoting. And maybe he was. He tried a toddler stomp around the stage. He rattled a pretend playpen, threw some pretend toys.

It didn't feel terrible. And two minutes wasn't so long.

As soon as the spotlight left him, Waylon pulled off the diaper. He was supposed to be a child next. For five minutes, the other kids encountered around him and he dug through his memories. Maybe he could emote a little bit more. Only a little bit.

Just as the spotlight picked him out again, a single day of his childhood popped into his head, crystal clear. His sixth birthday. That year, he'd wanted two things. Two things equally and desperately.

He'd gotten one of them: a microscope. Spit, dust, eyelashes, salt—everything went on a slide.

The world, he'd learned that week, was infinitely fascinating at every level. Remembering it now, Waylon felt his whole body expand in joy. He threw his arms out wide toward the audience.

It didn't feel bad at all.

But then he remembered: he hadn't gotten the other thing—one of those giant dancing balloon men he'd seen outside a car dealership.

The disappointment had crushed him, but

he hadn't let his family know. Now on the Rep stage, why not admit it?

Waylon staggered to the stage floor under the blow. On his knees, he threw out his arms to the left, to the right, becoming the blow-up man he'd wanted so badly. He snapped his head and jerked himself up, waving his whole body wildly from his rooted feet.

It felt pretty good.

And it electrified the rest of the cast. Their lights went on and they shot out their arms, two dozen balloon dancers encountering each other with abandon, spines weaving in the wind.

Waylon took the opportunity to search the audience. One dim shape in the front row might be his mother, and another might be Marliana, but it was too dark to be sure. The rest of the people were just a blur.

There were a lot of them, though—that he could tell.

And then it was his cue again. At this stage, Waylon's father had portrayed a man receiving his own baby. Waylon did not even want to think about having a baby. But maybe, he thought, maybe it was kind of like finally getting your own dog.

He gave Eddy the long-jump signal, and Eddy sailed into his arms. Looking down at the proof that he actually had a dog, where a year ago he hadn't, Waylon thought he actually might melt.

He let Eddy go when his spotlight dimmed, and watched his dog with pride. Dumpster Eddy had been born for the stage. Somehow he always managed to be exactly with the pair of kids picked out by the red flashlight. He never ran into the audience, never lay down for a scratch or a nap, never followed his nose backstage for those ham sandwiches—which Waylon was sure Eddy could smell, because Waylon himself could smell them.

He was so busy admiring his dog, the spotlight caught him by surprise. If he'd counted right, this was the final stage before death.

Reflection, his father had called this stage. So Waylon reflected:

About how embarrassed he'd been when Mrs. Fernman had called him out in class.

About how frustrated his mom's mystery had made him.

About the great thrill of being chosen for the Science Expo, and the great disappointment of not being able to attend, and the great worry about how Mitchell would do.

About how happy he was to have met Dumpster Eddy and Baxter, and how upset it made him every time he had to leave Eddy at the station.

All of this went into a single two-minute performance.

And it felt terrific.

When the spotlight snapped off, he collapsed onto the stage, panting and sweaty.

While the other kids encountered, he hung

the ugly gray skin over his shoulders.

At his cue, he moaned and writhed for a two whole minutes of the death stage.

The curtain swept closed. It was over.

And Waylon was shocked to find that he was sorry about that.

Except: it wasn't over! The other kids bolted into the wings and Waylon ripped off the toilet paper, stripped off the old gray skin, and curled himself into a ball.

The velvet curtain parted once more, and the spotlight found him. Waylon was reborn. And this time he did it right.

This time, Waylon let it rip.

And the audience went berserk.

17

Clementine hadn't let go of the vomiting thing. She stood behind the refreshment table pouring ginger ale from the five giant bottles she'd brought and showing people how to roll paper plates into cones. "To catch anything that might come up," she explained.

Waylon loaded a plate with sandwiches and potato salad and went to drag Eddy away from his fans. Kids were taking turns carrying him around like royalty and feeding him cold cuts, and it looked like they could keep at it all night. But Waylon knew he had to be firm.

"Sorry, boy, you can't stay. Mom's going to be here soon." He brought him over to a quiet spot and sat down to share his sandwich. When they were finished, Waylon led Eddy to Officer Boylen, who was going to take him back to the station. "See you after school tomorrow, boy," he promised.

Neon had talked some of the kids into cleaning up the stage, so the party hadn't really gotten going yet. Waylon selected another sandwich. While he was eating it, his mother came in. "You did a wonderful job," she started. "You really surprised me." She gave him a hug. "And so that was Dumpster Eddy?"

Waylon brightened with pride. "Yup, that's him. Wasn't he great? He's really smart."

"Well, I want to talk with you about him, in fact." And then a surprising thing happened. Mrs. Zakowski's eyes filled with tears.

Too late, Waylon remembered: He was still wearing the leotard! With the Eddy hairs on it! His mother's eyes were streaming from just that one hug with those few hairs.

He jumped up. "I'm sorry, Mom, I'm sorry!"

he called over his shoulder as he ran to the dressing room.

How could he have been so dumb? Waylon changed and did a thorough job of washing his face and hands and feet. He got back to the party just in time to see Mitchell arrive. He made a beeline to get the news. "Well???"

"It went great!" Mitchell said through a triumphant grin. "I presented to my science teacher and he gave me a B+. So I'm in— summer baseball!"

"Oh, good, but I meant . . . Dr. Geller. Did she show up? Did she like my project? Does she want to meet me?"

"Whoa, slow down, Science Dude!" Mitchell laughed. "Everybody really liked your project. But sorry, the Geller lady never showed up."

"Are you sure?"

"Positive. Sorry."

"That's too bad." But even as Waylon said it, he felt relieved.

The truth was, it wouldn't have been enough for Dr. Geller to see his project, no matter how impressed it made her. Waylon had wanted to *meet* her. He would have hated missing that. "Thanks anyway."

The cast party began to fill up. First with the clean-up crew, then with parents stopping in, then with some people from the audience.

Marliana wrapped Neon in a hug and welcomed her to the Rep community. "You're a member of the tribe, doll-face," she cooed. "Your brother, too, of course."

Even Principal Rice stopped in and Clementine got her wish—although Mrs. Rice's husband wasn't a husband, she was a wife.

"Eleanor, these are two of my students, Clementine and Waylon," Mrs. Rice said, introducing them to a pretty woman in a yellow dress. "I believe you may have heard me mention them once or twice."

People kept coming in until there were nearly fifty partiers toasting with soda cups and saying "Congratulations!" "Next stop, Broadway!" and "My favorite part was . . ."

Whenever anyone said that last thing, the cast obligingly re-created the scene in question. This went on for such a long time Clementine's father went out for five more liters of ginger ale.

The party was finally slowing down when the door opened once more and in walked Mr. Zakowski. He ran over to Neon and swung her around. "By the looks of things, I'm guessing *The Everything* was a big hit!"

Waylon saw his mom join them and he

hurried over, too. "How did it go in Hollywood?"

Mr. Zakowski raised both his thumbs. "Sold it!" He grabbed his family in a group hug. "It's a fair hunk of money," he said. "Looks like I've got a reprieve. Thank you for letting me stick it out."

Waylon stepped back. He liked to play a game called One Awesome Thing at the end of each day, and now was a good time. One Awesome Thing, of course, was that Neon's performance

was a hit. An Even More Awesome Thing was that his father had sold a screenplay. It had been an especially awesome day.

But then Mr. Zakowski looked at his wife and raised an eyebrow. "And how did your day go?" he asked in a voice Waylon thought sounded a little worried.

And suddenly Waylon felt worried, too. A *lot* worried.

Waylon's mom smiled. "Everything I'd hoped for," she said. "Now, why don't you and Charlotte go over there where they're taking the cast pictures? I'd like to speak to our son alone."

Waylon's breath caught. Was his mother about to tell him she'd found a better family? And if so, why did she want to tell him alone? It didn't make sense.

And then it did.

18

"It was because of me, wasn't it?" he blurted out. "The secret thing you've been doing—it was because of me?"

Mrs. Zakowski looked surprised. "It was. How did you know that?"

Waylon hung his head. He couldn't look at his mother's face. "Neon and I figured it out. But we didn't know it was just me. We thought it was because of all of us, because we've all been gone. Dad's been so busy with his screen-play, Neon with her production, me with Eddy."

"Well, it's true that it's been pretty lonely around our place. But the others were temporary. Your dad and your sister will be back to normal next week. But you: you're going to have that dog all the way through school—for the next eight years at least. I couldn't take eight more years of that."

Waylon swallowed hard and raised his head. "So you . . . you found another family? Because of me?"

"What? Another family?"

"In the blue car," Waylon said miserably. "The man and the two kids in the backseat. Oliver and Maggie. We found the blond hairs on your sweater. Neon and I, we know."

"Oh no! Oh no, no, no!" Waylon's mom threw her arms around him. "No, you do not know. So, let me tell you." She dropped to her knees to look straight into his eyes. "You said something last winter. You were heading out to build your dog an igloo, and you said that when you grew up, you were going to invent an anti-dog-allergy pill.

"And that got me thinking. Why should I wait that long? Here we live in Boston, Massachusetts, with maybe the greatest concentration of scientists in the world. I checked around and found a lab experimenting with allergy reversal and—long story short—I talked my way into a trial. For months now, I've been taking shots every day."

"Shots?" Waylon rubbed his arms and shuddered at the thought of it. "I can't believe you did that for me."

"Oh, you can't? Look." Waylon's mom pointed to where Neon and Mr. Zakowski were hamming it up for the photographer. "Look at their faces. They're both so happy because of you. Your dad went to Hollywood and Neon's performance was a hit, all because you gave up the Expo. A few shots don't begin to measure up to how painful I know that was for you. Besides, I think I mostly did it for me."

"Really? You want a dog, too?"

She threw back her head and laughed. "No, silly!" Then her face went serious. "I mean, sure . . . but what I really want is *my son*. I've been missing you."

Waylon steeled himself. "So, what about the other family?"

Mrs. Zakowski sat

back on her heels. "The past week, I've been conducting a little experiment. One of the guys at the lab, Martin, has a dog—a golden retriever named Maggie. I've been going to his place after work every day to play with her. He has a little boy, Oliver. Martin brings me home every evening with Oliver and Maggie in the car. Maggie *the dog*. You thought it was a little girl? Well, I guess, from the back . . ." She gave a little chuckle.

Waylon almost laughed with her. Almost. "What about the secret circle on the calendar?"

"Today was my doctor's appointment to test how the experiment came out. I didn't tell you because I didn't want to disappoint you if it didn't work."

Waylon was half-afraid to hear the answer, but he had to know. "So? What did the doctor say?"

"She said . . ." Waylon's mom stood up. A slow grin slid over her face. She waggled her fingers in happy air quotes. "'Go get that dog.'"

Waylon gasped. "You mean . . . I can . . . Dumpster Eddy?"

"Doctor's orders. Let's go get that dog."

"Right now?" Waylon looked at his watch. "At almost eleven?"

"I think you've waited long enough. So let's go get that dog of yours."

Waylon suddenly couldn't speak. But Neon had come up next to them, and she sure could.

"You heard Mom," she cried. "Let's get that dog!"

"Get that dog!" repeated Waylon's dad.

"Get that dog!" chorused Mitchell and Clementine and Baxter and Marliana. In a few minutes, the theater rafters were shaking with the roar: "Get that dog!"

Of course, Waylon knew that sound was actually a wave of vibrations, but he had never experienced its true power before. He pumped his fist. "Get that *dog!*" he shouted with the others, and the words became a tidal wave of sound, strong enough to sweep nearly fifty people out of the theater and onto the street under a starry June sky in the middle of Boston, Massachusetts.

Waylon turned to the crowd behind him. "What are we going to do?" he cried.

And *Get that dog!* was a mighty enough wave to roll right down Huntington Avenue, growing louder and more joyful with each block. The wave crested at the police station, washing Waylon and his family up the steps.

Dumpster Eddy was already at the big front doors, barking his head off.

The entire police night shift was at the doors, too, ready to subdue whatever band of dangerous desperados Eddy might be barking his head off about. Baxter pushed his way to the front and waved the secret police All's-Well hand signal at them, and they unlocked the doors.

Waylon ran in and scooped up his dog. "Thanks for keeping him," he called to the night dispatcher as he spun back out the door, "but I'm bringing him home now. Forever!"

Waylon lay awake, watching the clock click off the minutes to midnight. He had Field Day in the morning, but he wasn't worried about being tired. He didn't think he'd ever be tired again. How could he ever feel tired when he had his own dog lying right in bed with him?

Eddy squirmed and put his paws up over his ears.

Waylon remembered what the night dispatcher had said. He reached down and stroked Eddy's silky ears and immediately, Eddy sighed a whole-body *woof* of relief.

Just then, Waylon heard the softest knock on his door. "I'm awake," he answered.

Waylon's mother came in carrying two fancy cut-glass dishes of pudding. She handed one to Waylon with a spoon. "Special night. Plus, I figured you be hungry."

She was right. He was starving again. He dug his spoon in and ate.

His mom sat at the end of the bed. "I'm sorry you were worried before," she said after a few bites. "I can't believe you thought I wanted to be with a different family."

"I asked you. You wouldn't tell."

She pointed her spoon at him. "I'm a little tiny bit disappointed, too. It's not good science to leap to a conclusion without testing out any more theories. Without doing your research."

Waylon finished his dessert and then held the almost-empty dish out to Dumpster Eddy.

His mother covered her eyes, laughing. "Okay. As long as I don't see it, it doesn't happen. That will be our deal," she said.

While Eddy licked the dish spotless, Waylon reflected. What his mom said about his flawed reasoning was true. Maybe it was best he hadn't met Dr. Geller. He had a long way to go to be a great scientist.

As if she'd read his thoughts, his mom asked, "Are you terribly disappointed?"

"No. Mitchell said Dr. Geller didn't show. I guess it was pretty stupid to think I'd ever

195

actually meet her. Besides . . ." Waylon reached down and lifted Eddy onto his stomach. He was suddenly so tired he could barely speak. But he had one more thing to add.

"Besides," he said. "My dog. The Most Awesome Thing of All."

THE END

(almost)

Friday morning, Waylon woke up ravenous, as usual. Eddy woke up ravenous, too, so after Waylon dropped his bread into the toaster, he shook out a bowl of kibble.

Just then, Neon cruised into the kitchen. She caught Waylon's toast as it popped up and she reached for a plate.

Waylon put up a palm. "No," he said. And he meant it.

Neon looked at her brother as if she were seeing him for the first time. She considered the toast. She put it on the plate and handed it over. "Whatever," she said. "Thanks for last night."

She dug into her pocket and pulled out an envelope. "Which reminds me. Someone left this for you at the theater."

The envelope was addressed TO THE BOY IN THE PINK LEOTARD. Waylon had hoped he would never be reminded of that fake-naked costume again, and he was tempted to drop the envelope in the trash.

But he was a scientist, and scientists are curious.

Waylon opened it and drew out a Beantown Rep brochure. On the back was a note, handwritten in green ink. Waylon read:

To Whomever You May Be,

It was a privilege to watch the presentation of "The Everything" tonight. Chief among its pleasures for me was your extraordinary performance.

You expressed an entire range of human emotional experience, which struck me as being similar to the exploration of our galaxy, only internal. I was quite moved: an entire galaxy of human experience in the space of half an hour, its movements eloquently mapped out by toilet paper.

I have no idea if you are interested in science, but allow me to invite you to my presentation at the Hayden Planetarium Friday evening. Enclosed please find two tickets, front-row seats. I will try to entertain you as well as you entertained me, and I look forward to meeting you afterward.

Yours in the Cosmos,
Dr. Margaret J. Geller

Don't miss the first two

WAYLON! One Awesome Thing

★ "Alternately laugh-aloud funny and melt-your-heart tender, this illustrated chapter book is a great read aloud choice and a memorable find for independent readers."
—*Booklist* (starred review)

★ "Sara Pennypacker's style of creating true-to-life characters that readers instantly bond with will make readers fall in love with Waylon. Fans of Clementine will love this book."
—*School Library Connection* (starred review)

★ "In Pennypacker's skillful hands, Waylon is an appealing everykid whose passion for science just might spark readers' curiosity as he contemplates ideas from angstroms to alien hand syndrome. A winning, welcome new series for chapter book readers."
—*School Library Journal* (starred review)

books about Waylon!

WAYLON! Even More Awesome

SARA PENNYPACKER

Waylon!
Even More
Awesome

PICTURES BY
Marla Frazee

"Once again, Pennypacker offers an involving
early chapter book with well-developed characters
and a story line that feels both fresh and timeless. . . .
[A]ppealing black-and-white illustrations give the
pages an inviting look, while Waylon's dilemmas,
actions, and reflections will draw readers
into this satisfying narrative."
—*Booklist*

"Side story lines involving collaboration at school and
at home bring more nuance and meaning to Waylon's
dilemmas. Waylon still loves science and shares
surprising facts whenever he can. . . . Clementine, star
of Pennypacker's previous series, makes a few helpful
cameos, with her straightforward outlook and creative
spirit. Frazee's illustrations deftly capture the story's
funniest as well as most meaningful moments."
—*The Horn Book*

Clementine

★ "Fans of Judy Moody will welcome this portrait of another funny, independent third-grader."

—*Publishers Weekly* (starred review)

★ "Frazee's engaging pen-and-ink drawings capture the energy and fresh-faced expressions of the irrepressible heroine. . . . A delightful addition to any beginning chapter book collection."

—*School Library Journal* (starred review)

The Talented Clementine

★ "Clementine is a true original. . . . Libraries will need multiple copies of this one, because early chapter-book readers will jump at the chance to spend another eventful week with Clementine."

—*School Library Journal* (starred review)

★ "Pennypacker once again demonstrates her keen insights into the third-grade mind with Clementine's priceless observations of the world around her."

—*Kirkus Reviews* (starred review)